For Papa Wale, who gave
medicine away for free
until he was poor himself.
My uncle, my teacher,
my inspiration.
A.

For Jacky P, and team Bear
L.T.

Love from ANNA HIBISCUS!

by Atinuke

illustrated by Lauren Tobia

WALKER
BOOKS

First published 2015 by Walker Books Ltd
87 Vauxhall Walk, London SE11 5HJ

6 8 10 9 7 5

Text © 2015 Atinuke
Illustrations © 2015 Lauren Tobia

The right of Atinuke and Lauren Tobia to be identified as author and illustrator respectively of this work has been asserted by them in accordance with the Copyright, Designs and Patents Act 1988

This book has been typeset in StempelSchneidler and Lauren

Printed and bound by
CPI Group (UK) Ltd, Croydon, CR0 4YY

British Library Cataloguing in Publication Data:
a catalogue record for this book is available from the British Library

ISBN 978-1-4063-4912-2

www.walker.co.uk

MIX
Paper from
responsible sources
FSC® C020471

ABC and 123

Anna Hibiscus lives in Africa. Amazing
Africa. She lives in a big white house in a big
busy city with her whole entire family.

But Anna Hibiscus is not in the city now.
She is on holiday with Grandmother and
Grandfather and her big girl cousins, Joy
and Clarity and Common Sense. They are
visiting the village where Grandmother and
Grandfather were born.

Anna Hibiscus loves the village. She plays with her village friends all day long. But Anna Hibiscus has to work as well! There is too much work in the village for the mothers and fathers to do alone. The children have to help too!

Every single day Anna Hibiscus and her village friends take the goats to graze in the hot bush. While they are watching over the goats they play and laugh. And they learn too! The village children are teaching

Anna Hibiscus new songs and new games and how to fire a catapult well-well.

And Anna Hibiscus is teaching the village children ABC and 1,2,3. Anna Hibiscus loves to teach her friends. But now her friends are asking her questions that she cannot answer!

"What is 46 plus 92?" Tosin shouts.

"What is 23 minus 16?" Tolu shouts.

"What is the spelling of 'anthill'?" Beni shouts.

"Grandfather, what is 46 plus 92?" asked Anna Hibiscus when she was back in their compound.

"Grandmother, what is 23 minus 16?" asked Anna Hibiscus.

"Clarity, what is the spelling of 'anthill'?" asked Anna Hibiscus.

"Ummm," mumbled Grandfather, writing the numbers on the ground.

"Seven," said Grandmother.

"Oh, Anna Hibiscus," sighed Clarity. "Why are you asking these questions every-every night?"

"Is it your homework?" asked Grandmother.

"Is it too difficult for you?" asked Grandfather.

"I thought you only had spellings to learn," said Clarity.

"It is not homework," Anna Hibiscus said. "It is my friends, Tosin, Tolu and Beni! They are only small but they are asking me such difficult questions."

The big girl cousins burst out laughing.

"The pupils are too clever for the teacher!" said Clarity.

Anna Hibiscus frowned. Grandfather tried not to smile.

"Tomorrow your cousins can go and help you teach your friends," he said.

Joy and Clarity and Common Sense stopped laughing.

Every single day the big girl cousins went to the river to wash clothes. All the other big boys and girls in the village went too. They had a lot of fun there.

But the very next day, instead of going to the river, the big girl cousins had to go to the hot-hot bush with Anna Hibiscus, the small children and the smelly goats.

"How do you spell 'crocodile'?" shouted Tosin.

"How do you spell 'snake'?" shouted Tolu.

"How do you take a big number from a small number?" shouted Beni. "It is not possible!"

Joy and Clarity groaned. Common Sense eyed the village children. Some were quite big. Others were quite small. They were scattered all around, shouting out their questions.

"Silence!" yelled Common Sense.

Everybody looked at her.

"Stand together with your age mates!" Common Sense shouted. "With those born in the same year as you."

The village children started moving around.

"If you were born in the year the river flooded the fields, come and stand next to me," Common Sense said.

"Stand with Clarity if you were born in the year the chief's roof caught fire," she continued.

"If you were born in the year that the wild pigs trampled the fields, then come here!" Joy called.

"I will teach you big ones," Common Sense said to the children standing next to her.

"I will teach you," Clarity said to her group of medium-sized children.

"And I am your teacher." Joy smiled at the smallest children.

Anna Hibiscus frowned. This was

too much like school! Any minute now Common Sense was probably going to make them sit down and be quiet.

"Sit down!" shouted Common Sense. "And be quiet! If you have a question put up your hand."

"Come on, Anna!" called Clarity. "You are in my class."

Anna Hibiscus shook her head. Everybody in Clarity's group was smaller than she was!

"Don't cause trouble, Anna!" shouted Common Sense. "Do as you are told."

Anna Hibiscus did as she was told. But she was annoyed. Anna Hibiscus complained when they got back to their compound.

"They made me sit with small children!"

"What is this?" asked Grandmother.

"We didn't!" said Joy. "I was teaching the little ones. Anna was with Clarity."

"They were still smaller than me!" said Anna.

"Maybe smaller," said Clarity, "but not younger."

"They were all born the year the chief's roof caught fire," said Common Sense. "The same year as Anna Hibiscus."

Anna Hibiscus opened her mouth to argue. But Grandmother spoke first. "I remember it so well," she said. "It was hot that year. The rains were late. Your mother was waiting and waiting for you to be born, Anna Hibiscus. And the day you came, the rains came too. It was wonderful! Wonderful!"

Grandfather joined in. "The very day you were born, the chief's roof caught fire. His whole palace would have burned down but the rains started at that very moment. The very moment you were born, Anna Hibiscus.

That is why your name is
Anna Hibiscus Iyanu."

"Iyanu means 'Miracle'."
Grandmother smiled.

Anna Hibiscus was
amazed. Grandmother
and Grandfather had
given her a lot to think
about. She had never

heard about the day she was born, or about
the rain, or the chief's fire!

It was only when they had finished eating
that Anna Hibiscus remembered
what had been troubling her.

"But if Tosin and Tolu
and Beni are my own age,
then why are they all so
much smaller than me?"
she asked.

Grandmother sighed. She shook her head.
"Time to wash the bowls," she said.

16

"Ore mi, no," said Grandfather. "We must answer Anna's question. We cannot avoid the truth."

"Even when it stings like a scorpion?" asked Grandmother.

"It is better to face the scorpion prepared than be stung unawares," Grandfather said.

He looked at Anna Hibiscus.

"You are a lucky girl, Anna Hibiscus," he said. "You eat breakfast and lunch and dinner every single day."

"Yes, Grandfather," said Anna Hibiscus.

"Well, that is the reason that you and your classmates in the city are so big and strong," said Grandmother. "Simple as that. Now let us wash the bowls."

Anna Hibiscus looked at Grandmother. Then she looked at Grandfather. She still did not understand.

Grandfather looked sad. "Here in the village, people are poor," he said. "They eat only once a day. Sometimes not even that."

"You are bigger than the children here because you can eat whenever you are hungry," continued Grandmother, "and they cannot."

"Your friends do not have enough food to grow as big and tall as you, Anna Hibiscus," added Clarity.

Anna Hibiscus was so shocked she could not speak. She could not believe that her friends had so little food they could not grow big!

Anna Hibiscus started to cry.

Grandmother and Grandfather looked sadly at Anna Hibiscus. The big girl cousins put their arms around her.

"Crying is not going to help your friends," said Common Sense kindly.

"But how can I help them?" Anna Hibiscus sobbed.

"You cannot," said Clarity sadly. "We have not got enough food to feed them all."

"You can help them by being their friend," said Joy.

"That won't help!" said Anna Hibiscus.

When it was time to say goodnight, Anna Hibiscus would not speak.

"What's wrong, Anna?" asked Grandmother.

"My friends are hungry and I cannot help them," Anna Hibiscus said.

"Are you sure you can't help?" asked Grandmother.

Anna Hibiscus nodded. "We have not got enough food to feed them all," she said.

Grandmother took Anna Hibiscus's face between her hands. She looked into Anna Hibiscus's eyes.

"We may not have enough food to feed them but you can still help them," Grandmother said. "Anything is possible, Anna Hibiscus. Anything at all."

But Anna Hibiscus only cried.

All that day, and the next day, and the next day, Anna Hibiscus stayed in the compound. When she heard her friends calling her she hid in the house.

"Has Anna Hibiscus gone home?" the village children asked Grandfather on the first day.

"Is Anna Hibiscus sick?" the village children asked Grandmother on the second day.

"Does Anna Hibiscus not like us any more?" the village children asked the big girl cousins on the third day.

Grandmother shook her head. Grandfather shook his head. The big girl cousins shrugged their shoulders. They could not answer for Anna Hibiscus, but they could speak to her.

"Anna Hibiscus," Joy said gently, "your friends think that you don't like them any more."

"If you don't play with them," said Common Sense, "they will think they did something wrong."

"It is not their fault that they are hungry," said Clarity. "And it is not your fault that you are not, Anna."

Anna Hibiscus said nothing. But Anna Hibiscus listened.

The very next day Anna Hibiscus went
to herd goats with the village children. But
Anna Hibiscus did not smile. She did not
laugh. She did not play.

The village children looked sadly at Anna
Hibiscus. For so many days she had not come
out of her compound. And now she had a
face as long as a donkey's. What was wrong?

The children walked slowly through the
bush. None of them wanted to laugh or joke
or play.

They came to the place where they
always stopped to rest. There were big

rocks to climb on. And trees to give shade.
The goats spread out to eat the dry grass.

"Teach us, Anna!" begged Beni.

Anna Hibiscus pressed her lips together
and shook her head. What use was ABC and
1,2,3 to children who were hungry?

Slowly Tosin started to clap her hands
and stamp her feet. All of the girls watched.
Faster and faster she clapped and stamped.
It was a rhythm that made
Anna Hibiscus
want to dance!

Suddenly Tosin
stopped. Now
it was the other
girls' turn. It was
their turn to copy
exactly what
Tosin had done.
If not, they were
out of the game.

Anna Hibiscus loved this game! She stopped thinking about what was wrong. She watched the game, and smiled.

Beni saw Anna smiling. When the game was finished he shouted, "Anna Hibiscus! Look at this!"

Beni aimed his catapult at a guava high in a tree. As the guava fell, Tolu caught it. She brought it to Anna Hibiscus. Everybody knew that guavas were Anna Hibiscus's favourite fruit.

Anna Hibiscus smiled.

Beni held out his catapult.

"You try," he said.

Anna shook her head.

"Come on!" begged Tosin.

"Come on!" begged Tolu.

"Come on!" begged Beni.

Slowly Anna Hibiscus took the catapult. She aimed at another big guava in the tree. But Anna Hibiscus missed the tree completely. The tiny stone hit a goat busy chewing a bush. The goat stopped chewing and turned around to look at Anna Hibiscus.

"*Baaaaaaa!*" the goat reproached Anna Hibiscus.

Beni covered his mouth to stop from laughing. But the other children laughed. And Anna Hibiscus laughed too!

Anna Hibiscus laughed so hard she had to hold on to a tree so that she did not fall down.

The children tried to stop laughing but the goat said "*Baaaaaaa!*" again and glared at Anna Hibiscus.

The children laughed until they had to hold on to their stomachs.

"Anna Hibiscus," they gasped, "that goat is not going to forget you."

Then Beni said, "Nobody is going to forget you, Anna Hibiscus."

"No," agreed Tosin. "None of us will forget you. When you are with us, I am so busy laughing that I forget that my baby sister is so heavy."

"And when I am busy remembering ABC, then I forget how hot the bush is!" said Beni. "And how hungry I am."

"And how my mother is always shouting and shouting at me," said Tolu.

"Instead," said Tosin, "I think how clever I am. So clever that I am going to be a lawyer."

"I will have a big farm," said Beni. "When I can read I will learn all about new irrigation methods. My farm will feed many people. We will never be hungry again."

Beni smiled at Tosin.

"And nobody will take the farm away from me, because my good friend Tosin will be my lawyer," he said.

"I want to become a teacher," said Tolu. "But you will have to keep teaching us,

Anna Hibiscus, or it will never happen."

Anna Hibiscus stared at her friends.
She could not believe her ears. She had
been helping. She had been helping them
all along!

"OK," Anna said. "Le's go! Who can
remember their A to Z?"

"A to Z?" laughed Tosin. "I can remember
how to spell 'opportunity'!"

"Na-wa-oh!" said Anna Hibiscus, laughing.

Grandmother had been right. Anything
was possible. Anything at all.

Anna Hibiscus
Catches a Thief

Anna Hibiscus loves being in the village.
She loves hearing Grandfather laugh under
the iroko tree with his old friends. She loves
helping Grandmother make the delicious
breakfasts. She loves herding goats with her
new friends in the bush.

But most of all Anna Hibiscus loves to go
to market. She loves walking in the long line
of village women and children. She even
loves carrying the heavy basket of shopping
all the way home.

The market is in a different village.
Anna Hibiscus meets new children there.
She learns new games, sings new songs and
hears new stories. Anna Hibiscus is always
very busy at market!

"Anna Hibiscus!" called Joy at the end of
the morning. "It is time to go."

"We have done all the shopping," said
Clarity.

"Now it is your turn to help!" said
Common Sense.

Anna Hibiscus said
goodbye to her market
friends. She ran to
where her cousins were
waiting, each with a
big basket of shopping
on her head. There
was a little basket of
fruit waiting for Anna
Hibiscus to carry.

But when Anna
Hibiscus picked up her
basket, a small dirty
hand appeared and
snatched a banana.

Anna Hibiscus
couldn't believe it!
She saw a small boy
running away with
the banana.

"Thief!" Anna Hibiscus
shouted. "Thief! Thief!"

Anna ran straight
past her cousins after
the boy.

"Stop, Anna!"
shouted
Common Sense.

But Anna Hibiscus did not stop. She did not answer. Anna Hibiscus was chasing a thief!

She chased him in between the market traders. She chased him around the compounds. The boy was very fast. But Anna Hibiscus was angry. And that made her fast too!

The boy disappeared through a curtain hanging in a small doorway. Anna Hibiscus did not stop. She did not knock. She ran in after the boy.

Behind the curtain was a dirty room.
There was nothing in it at all. There was
only the boy holding the banana. He
was dusty and dirty and ragged.

"Give me my banana!" shouted Anna
Hibiscus.

The boy said nothing.

"Give me my banana!" shouted Anna
Hibiscus again. "You thief!"

"Anna?" The big girl cousins were calling
outside the curtain. "Is that you?"

"I am here!" Anna shouted.

The big girl cousins peeped around the curtain.

"What are you doing?" said Joy.

Anna Hibiscus pointed at the boy. "This is the thief who stole our banana!" she said.

All of a sudden the boy turned to face the wall and started to cry.

"Anna! Come out!" said Common Sense sharply.

She took hold of Anna Hibiscus's arm and pulled her out of the room.

"Le's go," said Clarity.

"But what about that boy?" asked Anna Hibiscus. "He took our banana!"

The big girl cousins shrugged their shoulders. They pointed their feet in the direction of home. And walked. Anna Hibiscus followed them. She was even angrier now.

When they arrived home, Grandmother and Grandfather were sitting in the compound. They saw Anna Hibiscus's angry face.

"Waytin' happen?" they asked.

The big girl cousins told Grandmother and Grandfather about the small boy.

"I chased him!" said Anna Hibiscus proudly. "And I caught him!"

"She followed him into his house!" said Common Sense.

Grandmother and Grandfather looked at Anna Hibiscus.

"Anna Hibiscus," said Grandmother. "Did he ask you to follow him inside?"

Anna Hibiscus shook her head. Grandmother and Grandfather looked shocked.

"Anna Hibiscus!" said Grandfather. "It is wrong to go into somebody's house if they have not invited you!"

"But he was a thief!" argued Anna Hibiscus.

"Even so!" said Grandfather.

Anna Hibiscus frowned. She was not the one who had stolen a banana. But now she was the one who was in trouble!

"He still has our banana!" she said crossly.

Grandfather sighed. He reached for his stick. He pulled himself upright. He walked out of the house to the iroko tree. They all watched him go.

Through the window they could see Grandfather talking with his friends. Soon he was back. His face was very sad.

"That boy is Oluwalomo's grandson," he said to Grandmother. "My old friend Oluwalomo, who died last year."

Grandmother gasped.

"But they are a good family!" she said.

"What has happened to make the boy a thief?"

Grandfather's voice was sad too.

"Four years ago the boy's mother died of a sickness," he said. "The father had run away. So my friend Oluwalomo looked after his grandson. When he passed away last year the boy was left alone. I did not know."

"Alone?" asked Anna. "All alone?"

"Is there nobody else?" asked Grandmother. "Nobody else to look after him?"

"There is nobody." Grandfather shook his head. "The neighbours are too poor to take him in. They cannot even feed their own children. The boy is hungry. If he wants to eat, he has to steal."

Suddenly Anna Hibiscus remembered the boy's face when he turned away to face the wall.

Anna Hibiscus covered her own face with her hands.

"I will go there," Grandfather said. "I must go to see this boy."

Grandmother took Grandfather's hand.

"Ore mi," she said. "Your stick cannot carry you further than the iroko tree."

"But that boy is the grandson of my friend!" Grandfather's voice shook.

"I will go," Grandmother said. "I will take him food. My legs are younger than yours."

"I will cook the food," said Common Sense.

Anna Hibiscus swallowed her tears. "I will carry the food," she whispered.

Everybody looked at Anna Hibiscus.

"You are ready to carry food to a thief, Anna Hibiscus?" Grandmother asked.

"He is not really a thief," choked Anna Hibiscus. "It is only because he has nothing to eat."

Grandfather shook his head.

"He is still a thief," he said. "Only now you understand why he was stealing."

"Every person who does wrong has a story," sighed Grandmother. "If we knew their stories we would be sorry for all of them. We would carry food to all of them."

Anna Hibiscus looked at the ground. She wanted to cry. But it felt like a stone was stuck in her throat.

The next day Grandmother called the
cousins.

"This morning we make rice,"
she said. "Sweet
soft rice. And we
make palm-oil
stew. Good strong
palm-oil stew."

The big girl cousins cooked the good food.

They roasted
plantains
and yams
as well.
Then they
loaded a big pot of all the food onto Anna
Hibiscus's head.

Anna Hibiscus followed Grandmother
into the bush. When they came to the boy's
village, Anna Hibiscus led the way. They
stood outside the raggedy curtain that was
the door into the boy's house.

"Tock, tock," said Grandmother, pretending to knock.

There was a small noise in the house.

"I am a friend of your grandfather!" Grandmother called. "I have come with food."

The curtain opened. The boy's dirty face peered out. When he saw Anna Hibiscus he looked afraid. Anna Hibiscus felt ashamed.

"Can we enter?" asked Grandmother.

The boy hesitated. He looked at the pot on Anna's head.

"It is for you," Grandmother said gently. "Yam and rice and palm-oil stew."

The boy opened the curtain.

Grandmother entered and Anna Hibiscus followed. She put the pot of food on the ground. The boy did not ask them to sit down. He did not offer them water. He opened the pot and started to eat with his dirty hands. He stuffed the food into his mouth.

Anna Hibiscus looked at the floor. She wanted to find a way to say sorry. But the words were stuck like stones in her dried throat.

The boy finished eating. Grandmother told Anna Hibiscus to pick up the pot.

"In four days' time it will be market day," Grandmother told the boy. "We will bring more food."

The boy looked down.

"Thank you, ma," he whispered.

On market day Anna Hibiscus carried
another pot of food to the boy's house.

"Because my legs are the youngest,"
she said.

While Grandmother and the big girl
cousins were shopping, Anna stood alone
outside the boy's house.

"Tock, tock," she said.

The boy peered out from behind the
curtain. He looked at the pot of food.
But he did not look at Anna Hibiscus.

Anna Hibiscus went into the house.
She put the pot on the floor. She took

a deep breath.

"Sorry," Anna
Hibiscus said.
"Sorry that I called
you a thief."

43

The boy shrugged. He started to eat. Anna
Hibiscus swallowed.

"Sorry that I ran into your house," she
said.

The boy still did not look at Anna. He was
busy eating.

After a while Anna Hibiscus spoke again.

"Will you not take my sorry?" Her voice
wobbled.

The boy looked at Anna Hibiscus.
She looked very sorry.

"OK," he said. "I will
take your sorry."

By the time the boy
had finished eating,
Anna Hibiscus felt
a bit better.

"My name is
Anna," she said.
"Anna Hibiscus."

The boy looked surprised.

"I too have a double name," he said.

"For true?" asked Anna.

"Yes," said the boy.

He smiled shyly.

"My name is Sunny Belafonte," he said.

"Sunny Belafonte!" said Anna Hibiscus.

"I was named for my grandfather's favourite singer," Sunny said proudly. "Harry Belafonte."

Anna Hibiscus smiled.

"And I was named for my grandmother's favourite flower!" she said. "The Hibiscus."

Sunny Belafonte smiled too.

In the market Grandmother was busy
buying tomatoes. Clarity was busy
buying pineapples. Joy was busy buying
nail varnish. Common Sense was busy
buying rice.

All of a sudden they heard Anna

Hibiscus laughing.

They all looked up.

Anna Hibiscus

was running

through the market,

hand in hand with

the small boy who

had stolen their

banana. Both of

them were laughing.

Joy and Clarity and Common Sense
looked at one another. Then they looked
at Grandmother.

Grandmother raised her eyes and her
hands together.

On the way home the big girl cousins questioned Anna Hibiscus.

"What were you doing with that boy?" Joy asked.

"Playing," said Anna Hibiscus.

"But he is a thief," said Clarity.

"Last week you wanted to punish him," said Common Sense. "And this week you want to play with him. How is that possible, Anna Hibiscus?"

Anna Hibiscus looked at Grandmother. Grandmother winked.

"Anything is possible," Anna Hibiscus said. "Anything at all!"

Help Sunny!

Anna Hibiscus is still in the village. She is still on holiday. Today it is market day again. Anna Hibiscus is looking forward to playing with her new friend, Sunny Belafonte!

Anna Hibiscus was waiting in the compound with Grandmother. Grandmother was not coming to market today and Anna Hibiscus was waiting for her big girl cousins. She had Sunny Belafonte's pot of food ready on her head.

"Anna Hibiscus!" Joy shouted from inside the house. "Meet us outside the gate."

Anna Hibiscus heard the front door open. The big girl cousins were going out that way. Anna Hibiscus walked towards the compound gate. She would meet her cousins on the path outside.

"Joy!" Grandmother shouted. "Come here!"

"Grandmother, we are already late!" Joy shouted back.

"Now!" shouted Grandmother. "Immediately!"

Anna Hibiscus looked at Grandmother. Grandmother looked very annoyed. Joy and Clarity and Common Sense came slowly into the compound.

Anna Hibiscus's eyes opened wide.

Joy was wearing tiny-tiny pink shorts. You could see her legs all the way up and all the way down.

Grandmother shook her head slowly
and silently.

"Joy," she said at last. "Did you think that
you could go naked to market and I would
not find out?"

"I am not naked, Grandmother," Joy said.

"Your legs are naked!" Grandmother said
crossly. "And that is the same thing."

"I am wearing hot pants, Grandmother,"
Joy said. "Everybody wears hot pants."

"Nobody wears them in this village!" Grandmother snapped. "Do you want to shame your grandfather in front of his old friends?"

Joy looked at the ground.

"No, Grandmother," she said.

"Good," said Grandmother. "Go back inside and cover your legs properly with a long wrappa skirt. I want to see all of you in buba blouses and wrappa skirts and ..."

Grandmother looked at the big girl cousins' Afro hair styles.

"... headscarfs!"

"But, Grandmother!" Joy, Clarity and Common Sense groaned.

Grandmother did not answer. She crossed her arms and tapped her foot impatiently.

The big girl cousins went back into the house. When they came out again, each

and every one of them was wearing a neat blouse made of traditional African material. Their legs and heads were covered by matching material.

Grandmother nodded. "You can go now," she said.

Anna Hibiscus followed her cousins out of the compound. Grandfather entered. He looked fondly after his granddaughters.

"They are such good traditional girls," he said to Grandmother. "I am proud of them."

Grandmother smiled. "Of course," she said.

When they reached the market Anna Hibiscus went straight to Sunny Belafonte's house.

"Tock! Tock!" she said outside the curtain.

There was no answer.

"Tock! Tock!" Anna Hibiscus called loudly. "I's me! Anna!"

Sunny's neighbour poked her head out from behind her curtain. "Dat boy's sick," she said.

Anna Hibiscus stood outside Sunny's house. Should she go in? Last time she had done that Sunny had been very upset. And Grandmother and Grandfather had been angry. Anna Hibiscus did not want that to happen again.

Anna Hibiscus hesitated. She hopped from one foot to another.

"Sunny?" she called again.

There was still no answer. Anna Hibiscus did not know what to do! What if Sunny

was too sick to say "Come in"? Leaving
Sunny to suffer alone would be worse than
upsetting him.

Anna Hibiscus went in.

Sunny Belafonte was lying on the floor.
He was sweating.
And he was
shivering.
Anna
Hibiscus
touched
his arm.

"Sunny?" she whispered.

Sunny Belafonte did not answer. Anna
Hibiscus shook his arm. "Sunny!" she called
loudly.

Sunny Belafonte did not even open his
eyes.

Anna Hibiscus ran out of the house. She ran to the market. She found Common Sense.

"Sunny is sick!" Anna cried. "He is sick well-well! Come quick!"

Joy and Clarity and Common Sense ran with Anna Hibiscus back to Sunny's house. They looked at Sunny Belafonte lying on the floor. He was still sweating. He was still shivering. He was still silent.

The big girl cousins looked at one another. What should they do? Common Sense spoke to the neighbours.

"The boy's sickness no be small," she said to them. "He needs a doctor quick-quick."

The neighbours shook their heads.

"No doctor," they said. "No doctor here. Only medical centre."

They pointed in the direction of the road.

"Make you help us take him there?" Clarity asked.

The neighbours shook their heads again.

"Please!" Anna Hibiscus begged.

The neighbours disappeared back into their houses.

"I know where the medical centre is," said Joy.

"Me too," said Clarity. "But it is far."

"Too far for us to carry him there alone," said Common Sense.

"But we *have* to help Sunny!" Anna Hibiscus cried.

They all looked again at Sunny. Common Sense took a deep breath. "I will run and tell Grandmother and Grandfather," she said.

"I will run too," said Clarity. "Grandmother and Grandfather will know what to do."

Joy took a deep breath too. "I will carry Sunny to the medical centre," she said.

"Joy! Thank you!" Anna Hibiscus cried.

"Wait!" said Common Sense. "Wait to see what Grandfather says first."

"We cannot wait," said Joy. "Look at him."

Sunny was shaking now.

"He is too sick to wait," Joy said.

Joy bent down to pick up Sunny Belafonte.

"He is hot," she gasped. "Very hot."

"You should not carry him in the hot-hot sun," said Clarity.

Joy took off her headscarf.

Her squashed Afro was sticking up and
down in every direction.

"Joy!" Common Sense gasped. "Everybody
will see your messy hair!"

Joy shrugged. "I don't care!" she said.

Anna ran to wet the headscarf with
water from a bucket. She used it to cover
Sunny Belafonte. To protect him from the
hot-hot sun.

Joy carried Sunny Belafonte through the village and into the bush. She carried him through the bush to the road. Anna Hibiscus followed. The hot sun beat down on them. Sweat dripped down their backs and into their eyes. Red dust stuck to them. It stung their eyes and made their skin itch.

Suddenly Joy tripped. She almost fell down. She almost dropped Sunny Belafonte! Joy started to cry.

"It is too far!" she cried. "I cannot do it!"

Anna Hibiscus tried to help. But Sunny Belafonte was too heavy for her.

A car was coming. Anna Hibiscus jumped up and down by the side of the road. She shouted loudly and waved her arms.

"Stop!" she shouted. "Stop! Stop!"

The car slowed down.

"We need to go to the medical centre!" Joy shouted.

The driver looked at them. She started

to drive on. Then suddenly she stopped.
Anna Hibiscus and Joy ran after the car.
They climbed in with Sunny Belafonte.

Very soon they were at the
medical centre.

Anna Hibiscus thanked the kind driver.
Joy carried Sunny Belafonte into the
building. A doctor came and looked at him.

"He needs medicine now-now," she said.
"You have money for medicine?"

Anna Hibiscus
and Joy looked at
each other. Money?
They had no money!
Not enough for medicine!

"No?" said the doctor. "So put him there."

The doctor pointed to where many sick people were lying on the dirty floor. Anna Hibiscus grabbed the doctor's arm.

"Please!" she begged.

The doctor shook her head.

"I do not get medicine for free!" she said. "Somebody has to pay for it or I will not be able to buy more."

The doctor walked away. Anna Hibiscus started to cry. Joy looked for a place to lay Sunny down. But the floor was so dirty!

"Take off my wrappa," Joy said to Anna.

Anna Hibiscus hesitated.

"Hurry up!" Joy said.

Anna Hibiscus took off Joy's wrappa.

Underneath the wrappa Joy was still
wearing her tiny-tiny pink hot pants!

People stared at Joy. Some of them shook
their heads. Others rolled their eyes. But Joy
did not care. And neither did Anna Hibiscus.

Anna laid Joy's wrappa
on the dirty-dirty floor.
And Joy laid Sunny
on the clean
wrappa.

Anna Hibiscus knelt beside Sunny.
She had brought him all this long hot way
for nothing.

"Sorry, Sunny, sorry," Anna Hibiscus whispered.

Joy looked at Sunny Belafonte. She looked at Anna Hibiscus. Joy ran. She ran to find a telephone. Joy had enough coins for one telephone call. She phoned the big white house in the city.

"Hello." It was Uncle Bizi Sunday.

"Daddy! Daddy!" Joy was crying. The line was bad. There was so much crackling.

"Wha' happen? Wha' happen?" Uncle Bizi Sunday shouted.

"I am in the medical centre" – *crackle-crackle* – "Anna Hibiscus …!" Joy cried, "… very ill – unless we have medicine" – *crackle-crackle* – "die!"

"We are coming!" shouted Uncle Bizi Sunday.

The coins were finished. The line went dead.

In between the crackling, Uncle Bizi Sunday had heard that Joy was in the medical centre with Anna Hibiscus. He had heard that unless she had medicine, Anna was going to die!

Anna Hibiscus's mother and father jumped into their car. Auntie Grace and Uncle Bizi Sunday jumped in too. They drove fast to the medical centre. It still took them a long time to get there.

When they arrived they could not find Anna Hibiscus or Joy. The whole place was crowded with sick people and their relatives. People filled all the rooms and all the beds and all the floors.

Anna's father walked down the corridor.
He saw Anna Hibiscus lying on the floor.

"Anna!" he shouted.

Anna Hibiscus's mother ran down the
corridor. There was Anna Hibiscus lying
down next to a very
thin boy. Her arm
was around him.
Joy was sitting with
them, wearing
hardly any clothes.

Anna Hibiscus heard her father's voice!
She jumped up. She could not believe her
eyes. There were her mother and father!
Anna Hibiscus did not know what to say.

Then everybody spoke at once.

"Anna!" her mother cried. "Are you OK?"

"Did you bring money for Sunny Belafonte?" Anna Hibiscus asked.

"Joy!" said Uncle Bizi Sunday. "What is going on?"

There was a lot of explaining to do. In the end everybody was so glad Anna Hibiscus was not sick that nobody was cross about the mistake.

Anna Hibiscus was gladdest of all! "We have money for Sunny's medicine now!" she said.

"Anna..." said her father.

Anna Hibiscus looked at her father.

"Did you not bring money for medicine?" Anna Hibiscus was afraid now.

"But, Anna Hibiscus," said her father. "That money was for you. For medicine for you."

"But I don't need it." Anna Hibiscus was confused. "It is Sunny who needs it."

Anna's father took a deep breath.

"Anna Hibiscus," he said. "I have three children. My money is for my children. For medicine and clothes and school for you three."

Suddenly Anna Hibiscus could not breathe.

Uncle Bizi Sunday looked up and down the corridor. "We are a rich country," he said. "And look how we treat our poor people." He shook his head angrily. "People are dying on the floor so that others can have private helicopters and diamond rings."

Anna Hibiscus had never seen Uncle Bizi Sunday look so angry.

"Anna Hibiscus," Uncle Bizi Sunday

said, "here is some money for your friend. He needs it more than I need a new laptop."

Auntie Grace took out her wallet.

"He needs it more than I need a car." She smiled.

Anna's mother took out her wallet too.

"And more than I need a visit to Canada," she said.

Anna Hibiscus's father sighed.

"OK, OK," he said. "I will help too. But where are the people with private helicopters and diamond rings?" he asked. "They are the ones who should be helping these people!"

"They are not here," said Uncle Bizi Sunday.

"But we are here," said Anna Hibiscus.

Later that day, Anna Hibiscus sat on the
edge of Sunny Belafonte's clean bed.
She looked at the tubes carrying good
strong medicine into his arms. Then Anna
Hibiscus looked at her family. She looked
at her father and her mother, at her uncle
and her auntie and her cousin.

*I have the best family in the whole wide
world,* Anna Hibiscus thought. *And Sunny
Belafonte has no family at all. That is why he
needs us.*

Sunny Belafonte smiled at
Anna Hibiscus.

"Thank you," he said. "You are
the best friend in the whole wide
world."

Anything Is Possible

Anna Hibiscus is still in the village. But
Anna Hibiscus is no longer on holiday. Anna
Hibiscus is busy teaching her friends. She is
busy visiting Sunny Belafonte in the medical
centre. And she is busy worrying.

Sunny Belafonte has been very, very sick.
But he is almost better now. Anna Hibiscus
was not worrying about him. But she was
still worrying!

Grandfather caught sight of Anna's face. "Anna Hibiscus!"

He was sitting under the iroko tree with his friends.

Anna Hibiscus looked at Grandfather. She looked at the other elders sitting with Grandfather under the tree. They all looked so old and so wise. Surely Grandfather and his friends would know what to do about her worry.

"What is troubling you?" one of the elders asked.

Anna Hibiscus took a deep breath. Nobody was allowed to speak to the elders unless the elders spoke first. And the elders had never spoken to Anna Hibiscus before.

"I am worried about my friends," Anna said. "About Tosin and Tolu and Beni."

The elder chuckled.

"Why are you worrying about them?" he asked. "Are they not still surpassing you in mathematics and spelling?"

"Yes…" said Anna Hibiscus. "But who will teach them when I am gone?"

Another of the elders shrugged.

"How much ABC and 1,2,3 does a child need to know?" he asked.

Anna Hibiscus spoke up bravely.

"They need to know a lot," she said. "Because Tosin wants to be a lawyer. Tolu wants to be a teacher. And Beni wants to have a big farm and employ many-many people."

The elders looked surprised. Then they looked serious. They turned away from Anna Hibiscus and began to speak among themselves. Grandfather nodded to Anna Hibiscus and waved her away.

That night Grandfather wrote a letter. Joy posted it for him. Grandfather waited many days for an answer to his letter. An answer did not come.

Grandfather was concerned. "I need to make a telephone call," he said.

Grandfather walked to where he could find a mobile phone signal.

He used Joy's phone to make his call.

When Grandfather returned he looked old and small and tired. He stopped under the iroko tree. He spoke to his friends. They shook their heads and looked very sad. Grandfather returned to the compound.

"I have tried," he said. "I wrote to the minister of education. I told her our village needs a school. She did not answer me. Today I telephoned her office. I was told that she would not speak to me because she does not know me. I voted for her government but still she does not know me."

Grandfather's voice trembled. He went to lie down on his mat.

Now Anna Hibiscus was even more worried.

Anna Hibiscus was so worried that Sunny Belafonte noticed when she went to visit him.

"Anna Hibiscus!" said Sunny. "Wha's wrong?"

"Oh, Sunny!" Anna Hibiscus cried. "Soon I will go back to the city. And then who will teach my friends?"

Sunny Belafonte looked worried too.

"When will you go, Anna Hibiscus?" he asked.

"When you are better, Sunny," Anna said. "When you are better we will return to the city."

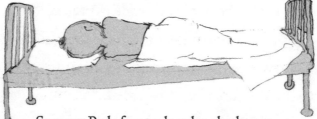

Sunny Belafonte lay back down on his bed. He turned to face the wall.

"Sunny!" Anna Hibiscus cried. "Wha's the matter?"

Sunny Belafonte did not reply.

Anna Hibiscus called the nurse. The nurse felt Sunny's head.

"You must go and let him rest," she said.

Sadly Anna Hibiscus whispered goodbye to Sunny Belafonte. She walked out of the medical centre.

"Ssss! Anna! Anna Hibiscus!"

Anna Hibiscus did not look around. She was too busy worrying!

"Ssss! ANNA HIBISCUS! STOP!"

It was Sociable and Thank God, Anna Hibiscus's big boy cousins. They were running after her and calling her name. Anna Hibiscus blinked. Sociable and Thank God were supposed to be at university in the city, not here in the bush.

"Anna Hibiscus!" Sociable was panting. "Wait for us!"

"Anna!" Thank God was laughing. "Do you not know your own cousins?"

Thank God picked Anna up and swung her through the air. Anna Hibiscus did not even smile.

"Wha' happen?" Thank God asked.

"Are you not happy to see us?" Sociable asked.

Anna Hibiscus hesitated. Every time she told somebody about her worries things got worse.

"Go on, Anna Hibiscus," said Sociable. "We may be big bad boys from the city but you can trust us!"

Anna Hibiscus looked at Sociable and Thank God. They did not look like big bad boys. They looked like her cousins. And she knew she could trust them. Slowly Anna Hibiscus told them the whole story.

"Unless they go to school, my friends will be hungry for ever," she said. "And the education minister won't even speak to Grandfather!"

"The education minister?" said Sociable.

"If she knew how clever my friends are, she would give them a school," Anna Hibiscus said. "They are more clever than me. I cannot answer even half of their questions."

Sociable and Thank God looked at each other.

"Are you thinking what I am thinking?" Sociable asked.

"Our university assignment?" asked Thank God.

"Great minds think alike, bro!" Sociable laughed.

The two cousins gave each other a big high-five. Anna Hibiscus crossed her fingers. Maybe this time things would be OK.

"We have an idea," said Sociable.

"A big idea," said Thank God.

Anna Hibiscus smiled. She liked big ideas.

Now whenever Anna Hibiscus went into the bush with her friends to herd goats, Sociable and Thank God went too. And they took their iPhones with them.

"Why are you always going into the bush?" Joy asked them.

"Why don't you come to the river with us?" asked Clarity.

"There are a lot of girls at the river," said Common Sense.

"Girls?" Sociable asked.

"No time for girls," said Thank God. "We are busy helping Anna Hibiscus."

Anna Hibiscus smiled. But she was still worried about Sunny Belafonte.

"He will not eat," the nurse had told her. "He will not drink. How can he get better if he will not eat or drink?"

Anna Hibiscus had wiped Sunny's face with a cool cloth. She had held his hand. She had tried to give him sips of water.

"Sunny," Anna Hibiscus had begged over and over again. "What is wrong?"

But Sunny Belafonte had not replied. He would not eat. He would not drink. He would not get better.

Back in the village Thank God and Sociable were happy. Thank God gave Anna a big thumbs up. And Sociable threw Anna into the air.

"I got the email from the newspaper today!" he said.

"It will happen tomorrow!" said Thank God.

Anna Hibiscus was excited to see if their plan had really worked. But when she saw

Grandfather sitting on his mat and looking sad, Anna looked sad too.

Grandmother went over to Anna Hibiscus. "Don't worry, Anna," she said. "Grandfather is disappointed that he could not get a school for the village. He will soon recover."

"Are you sure?" asked Anna Hibiscus.

Grandmother nodded and smiled. And Anna Hibiscus felt a little bit better.

"And Sunny?" she asked. "Will he recover too?"

"Sunny?" asked Grandmother. "I thought he was better."

"No," said Anna Hibiscus. "He is worse."

"Worse?" croaked Grandfather.

Anna Hibiscus told Grandmother and Grandfather the whole story.

"Maybe he is sad that there will not be a school," she said. "Because Sunny wants to be a doctor. He can't become a doctor without a school."

All of a sudden Grandfather smiled.

"Sociable!" Grandfather called. "Go to No. 1's village. Tell him we need him tomorrow."

Then Grandfather got up from his mat. And for the first time in many days he went to sit under the iroko tree with his friends.

Anna Hibiscus looked at Grandmother. She was too surprised to speak!

The next day Anna Hibiscus was even more surprised. A boy appeared outside the compound, leading cows that were towing an old Toyota Corolla.

"No. 1 is here in the Cow-rolla!" Sociable shouted.

Grandmother and Grandfather and Clarity and Common Sense and Joy and Sociable and Thank God all climbed into the Cow-rolla. Anna Hibiscus stood with wide open-eyes.

"You never see a Cow-rolla before?" The
No. 1 boy laughed.

"Never!" Anna Hibiscus shook her head.

"Tha's because i's my own invention!"
said the boy.

Anna Hibiscus was very impressed.

The No. 1 boy helped Anna Hibiscus
climb into the Cow-rolla. He told her all
about his many clever inventions.

"Na-wa-oh!" Anna Hibiscus laughed.

At the medical centre Grandmother and
Grandfather followed Anna Hibiscus to the
room where Sunny was lying.

"Ah, Sunny Belafonte! Grandson of my
good friend Oluwalomo," said Grandfather
loudly. "I hear that you want to become
a doctor."

There was no movement in Sunny
Belafonte's bed.

"I have always wanted to have a doctor

in the family," Grandfather continued.
"But my children wanted to be teachers
and engineers and accountants."

Grandfather sighed loudly. The stillness
in Sunny's bed was listening. Anna Hibiscus
was looking at the bed and she could tell.

"I am an old man," Grandfather said,
"too old to have more children of my own.
But I believe it is not too late to have a
doctor in the family."

"Will you help me, Sunny Belafonte?"
Grandfather asked.

Sunny Belafonte sat up.
He stared at Grandfather.
Anna Hibiscus stared too.

"How can I help
you, sir?" Sunny
Belafonte whispered.

"You can help me by coming to live in the
city with me and my family," Grandfather
answered. "You can help me by reminding
me of my dear friend, your grandfather, and
the good times we used to have together
when we were young. You can help me by
becoming the first doctor in my family."

Anna Hibiscus clapped her hands and
jumped up and down and up and down.

"Shhh," said Grandfather seriously.
"This is for Sunny Belafonte to answer."

Sunny Belafonte was still staring at
Grandfather.

Right then Sociable and Thank God
rushed into the room. They were shouting
and waving a newspaper.

"Look! Look!" they shouted.

Grandfather snatched the newspaper.

On the very front page there was a
big picture of Anna Hibiscus. She was
surrounded by her village friends. They
were all writing on the ground with sticks.

"'Small Village Headmistress!'"
Grandfather read. "'How One Small Girl
Took Things Into Her Own Hands
When the Government
Refused to Help.'"

"'By Sociable
Odogwu and Thank
God Anozie,'" read
Grandmother.

Grandmother and Grandfather looked at Sociable and Thank God. They looked at Anna Hibiscus.

"What is this?" Grandfather was astonished.

"We wanted to help Anna," Thank God said.

"And we had a journalism assignment for university," Sociable said.

"Maybe..." Anna Hibiscus started to explain.

Joy rushed into the room. She was holding out her mobile phone.

"Grandfather!" she said. "It is the minister for education! She wants to talk to you."

Grandfather closed his eyes.

"Tell her I am in a meeting," he said. Grandfather looked at Sunny Belafonte.

"A very important meeting," he said.

Sunny Belafonte looked at
Grandfather.

"Do you have an answer for
me, Sunny?" Grandfather asked.

"Yes, sir," Sunny Belafonte
said. "Yes, please, I will come
and live with you and help you.
Thank you, sir."

Grandfather's eyes shone. Anna Hibiscus's
eyes shone. And Sunny Belafonte's eyes
shone too.

"So you are going to eat now?"
Grandfather asked.

Sunny nodded.

"Because we have been waiting for you,"
said Grandfather. "We have been waiting
for you to recover so that we can all go
home together."

Sunny nodded once again.

"Good." Grandfather smiled.

Then he looked at the newspaper again.

"Young people," Grandfather shook his head. "You young people constantly amaze me."

Grandmother patted Grandfather's hand.

Anna Hibiscus looked at Grandfather. He was an old man. But he was a happy old man since they had come to the village. And now his eyes were shining with joy.

Anna Hibiscus looked at Sociable and Thank God. Their eyes were shining too. They were listening to Joy talking to the minister for education.

"A big school?" Joy was saying. "No problem! No problem! Yes, there are plenty of children here."

Anna Hibiscus smiled. She looked at Sunny Belafonte. He had the shiniest eyes of all.

"Thank you, Anna," he whispered.

Anna Hibiscus hugged Sunny Belafonte. He was part of her family now. She would never have to worry about him being sick or hungry or alone again. And he would never have to worry either.

What Grandmother had said was really true. Anything was possible. Schools. Medicine. Food. Families. Anything at all. It took money and time and knowledge.

But mostly, it took love.

Atinuke was born in Nigeria
and spent her childhood in both Africa
and the UK. She works as a traditional
oral storyteller in schools and theatres
all over the world. Atinuke is the author
of two children's book series, Anna
Hibiscus and The No. 1 Car Spotter.
Atinuke lives on a mountain overlooking
the sea in West Wales with her two sons.
She supports the charity
SOS Children's Villages.

Lauren Tobia lives in Southville,
Bristol. She shares her tiny house with
her husband and their two yappy
Jack Russell terriers. When Lauren is
not drawing, she can be found drinking
tea on her allotment.